Ginny's Egg

Also by Pippa Goodhart

Flow
The Lie Spider
Pest Friends
Frankie's House Tree
Time Swing
Alona's Story

Pippa Goodhart

Illustrated by Aafke Brouwer

Ginny's Egg

mammoth

For Nancy, a special friend

First published in Great Britain 1995
by William Heinemann Ltd
Reissued 2001 by Mammoth
an imprint of Egmont Children's Books Limited
a division of Egmont Holding Limited
239 Kensington High Street, London, W8 6SA

Text copyright © 1995 Pippa Goodhart
Illustrations copyright © 1995 Aafke Brouwer
Cover illustration copyright © 2001 Caroline Uff

The moral rights of the author, illustrator and
cover illustrator have been asserted

ISBN 0 7497 4557 6

10 9 8 7 6 5 4 3 2 1

A CIP catalogue record for this title
is available from the British Library

Printed and bound in Great Britain
by Cox & Wyman Ltd, Reading, Berkshire

Contents

Chapter One
AN ODD SORT OF EGG

Ginny picked up the egg. Its gold-speckled shell shimmered very slightly in the dim light that struggled through the dusty windows of the hen house. It was the size and shape of a pear, but more like an oversized tear drop, warm and fragile. In some strange way it seemed strong too.

As Ginny held the egg in her hand, she could feel it throbbing slightly. She took her thumbs away from the shell for a moment to test whether the throbbing came from her own thumb pulses beating onto the egg, but it didn't. The pulsing came from inside the egg. Ginny's tummy beat too and a cold tingle of excitement suddenly swept through her as she recognised what it was that she was feeling.

'You're alive, aren't you!' she said to the egg. 'There's a chick inside you.' Then she

7

looked at the egg again. 'But it can't be a hen chick. You're the wrong sort of egg.'

She held the egg's warmth to her cheek.

'You're the wrong colour and you're too big,' she told it. But what other sort of bird could have got into the hen house and laid the egg? Ginny looked around her at the high fox-proof fence of the hen run. Something could have flown down into the run from above, but it still didn't make much sense that it would lay its egg and then just leave it, did it? There were only Gran's six hens in the run now.

'You *must* be a hen egg, an odd sort of hen egg,' Ginny told it. Ginny often told herself sensible things, though she hardly ever really believed them. And today, however much a part of her wanted the excitement of a mystery egg, what she needed most was ordinary sense. She knew that the baby was about to be born and she didn't want any distractions from that.

'Think sense, Ginny Abbot. Gran's hens lay one egg each every morning.' She looked in the egg basket and counted. 'See! Five eggs and the one in your hand make six, and there are six hens. It's a hen's egg. Put it into the basket with the rest.'

But she couldn't ignore the feeling that this egg was different. Cradling the special egg between her hands, she crouched to look around the straw bales that the hens nested on. It didn't take long before she spotted the missing egg. 'There!' she said, and she wasn't sure whether she was pleased or cross to have found it.

Standing up with the two eggs in either hand, she compared them. The egg in her left hand had a dull ordinary shell but the one in her right hand shimmered. The ordinary eggs in the basket were for cooking with but the thought of breaking the special egg into a bowl and beating it up made Ginny feel quite ill. She lifted it up to tilt its shimmering shell in the light from the window.

'You're going to hatch out, and I've got to look after you, haven't I?' There was no choice. 'I'll have to keep you secret,' she said.

Ginny opened the soft pouch pocket on the front of her brown jacket and gently tipped the egg into it. Then she cradled it from the outside, guarding and nursing the egg with her hand. With her free hand Ginny scooped grain into the chickens' food trough and filled their water bowl. She had to let go of the precious pocket as she picked up the egg basket and opened the shed door. Quickly shooing the hens back in, she refastened the door and was glad to cradle the pocket again. Somehow, even though the pocket was deep and soft, the egg didn't feel properly safe unless she was holding it.

Ginny walked back up the garden to Gran's house. There had been a gale blowing last night. Small puffs of cloud still moved fast high up in a blue sky. The garden bore scars from the wind. Twigs and loose flower pots

scattered the lawn. It was as though some giant had taken a huge spoon and stirred it all round the garden, thought Ginny. She remembered lying awake last night and hearing the growing drumbeat of wind banging around the house, pulling at a loose clattery gutter and scratching twigs like witches' fingers on the window panes.

'I wonder if you were laid during that storm?' Ginny whispered down to her pocket. 'Could you hear the wind from inside your shell? Were you frightened?'

She looked around her at the windswept winter garden of greens and browns. A lot of

Gran's plants were dead, but tiny bright white snowdrops and golden yellow crocus heads waited patiently for the sun to fall on them before they would open out and show their full beauty. Like eggs waiting to hatch, thought Ginny and she frowned and felt again the weight in her pocket.

Gran stood waiting to meet Ginny at the back door.

'Are you all right, sweetheart?' she asked. 'You look as broody as one of my old hens! What have you got on your mind? Is it Mum and the baby?'

'Sort of,' said Ginny. The truth was that she hadn't thought about the baby since she had decided to take the egg, but Mum and the baby made a good excuse to talk about something else.

'Yes,' she said. 'Mum's been having backache and pains all morning and Dad's stayed home from work. They think that the baby might be coming.' Saying that brought all that other excitement fluttering back to her. A baby brother or sister at last!

'I know!' said Gran and she ruffled Ginny's

springy hair. 'Mum telephoned me. I was just coming to tell you that she wants you home now to say goodbye. They'll be off to the hospital soon.'

Ginny didn't wait. She thrust the basket of eggs into Gran's hands and was off.

'I'll follow as soon as I've locked up here,' Gran called after her, but Ginny didn't answer.

Gran chuckled to herself as she watched Ginny race off down the road, her twiggy nine-year-old's legs looking hardly strong enough to carry her.

'Oh, Ginny, you are a funny one,' said Gran to Ginny's disappearing back. 'You look like a flustered mother hen!' Then Gran noticed that Ginny ran lop-sidedly. One arm swung free but the other was clamped to her tummy. Perhaps a tummy-ache was what had been bothering her?

Gran picked a few snowdrops and added them to the eggs in the basket before going back into the house.

Chapter Two
BOTTOMS

It didn't take Ginny long to run down the road from Gran's house to her own home. When she raced through the back door she found Mum sitting in the kitchen, a bit pale and a bit shiny-eyed and with her hands resting on her bulging stomach.

'You're in a hurry!' she said as Ginny raced in. 'Take your jacket off, love, and have some breakfast with me before we go. They'll starve me at the hospital – I remember that from last time – so Dad is doing me some toast and honey. Would you like some?'

Then something gripped tight inside Mum and she clutched the chair seat and panted. Ginny hadn't realised that it would hurt Mum so much having the baby, but Mum and Dad looked happy so she supposed that everything was all right.

'OK, Maggie?' asked Dad, gently stroking

Mum's head. Ginny smiled when she saw that he had cut the toast and honey into soldiers as he had used to do for her when she was little.

'Don't you laugh at your old dad!' he told her. 'We need to look after Mum. She's got a big job ahead of her.'

Mum blew out as if to blow away the pain that had held her a moment before. 'I'll eat my honey soldiers all up like a good girl!' she laughed, and she and Dad smiled together.

Ginny began to unbutton her jacket, and then she remembered – the egg.

'Oh!' she said aloud.

'What is it?' asked Dad.

'Oh, nothing. I'll be down again in a minute.' She ran out of the room and up the stairs. It was so annoying! She didn't want to have to bother with the silly egg when Mum was about to have their baby! But she couldn't hang up the jacket downstairs. The egg could easily get squashed and broken.

Up in her room, Ginny yanked her jacket off quite roughly but she put her hand into its pocket more gently. As she touched the egg and felt again its warm hum of hidden life, she knew why she had taken it. It was hers to care for.

Ginny arranged her jacket into a ring shape on her bed. It was still warm from her body and would keep the egg warm while she said goodbye to Mum and Dad. She gently placed the egg in the centre of the jacket nest.

'See you soon,' she promised as she headed back to the stairs, and then laughed quietly at herself for talking to an egg.

Back in the kitchen Mum was eating her honey soldiers and trying to organise. 'Remember that tomorrow is dustbin day and . . .'

Dad was writing the hospital's phone number down for Ginny and Gran.

Mum looked at her watch. 'And then we must go, Stephen,' she said.

'Yes, love,' assured Dad. 'Everything's ready and I can see Gran just coming down the road.'

Ginny suddenly realised that this was the last time it would be just her and Mum and Dad.

'Can we do "Bottoms"?' she asked. 'We haven't done that for ages!'

'Oh, yes,' said Mum. 'One last time before we have a tiny new bottom to join the gang!' and she heaved herself bulkily out of her chair.

'Bottoms' was a silly family chant that had started when Ginny was four and full of questions. She had asked, 'Dad, what is a "bot"?'

Dad had looked puzzled but answered, 'Well, I suppose that bot must be short for bottom and a bot must be one bottom, or possibly the first bottom since "a" is the first letter of the alphabet. Why?'

And Ginny had said, 'Because that's us!' Dad had still looked blank so Ginny had explained, 'It's our name, silly! Abbot – a bot!'

And out of that had grown the Bottoms ritual that Mum and Dad and Ginny did, usually when they were saying goodbye or celebrating coming back together again, but never in public. All three of them would stand back to back and bump their bottoms together as they chanted,

17

'Daddy "A" bot, Mummy "B" bot,
Ginny "C" bot,
As you can *see*, we're a fami*ly* of one,
two, *three* – Bottoms!'

And then they twizzled round and joined arms in a three-cornered hug.

They did it now and the hug was stretched almost beyond Ginny's reach by Mum's great tummy.

'What are you all up to?' laughed Gran as she came in and caught them in the middle of it.

'Oh,' said Mum. 'We were just doing "Bot–",' but then she sucked in her breath as another pain clenched her. She leaned on Dad and puffed and panted her way through it while Dad rubbed her back and they rocked gently together. Ginny held Mum's hand and as the pain passed Mum winked encouragingly at Ginny's worried face.

'Take care of Ginny for me,' she told Gran. 'And I promise we'll ring with news as soon as there is any.' She saw Ginny open her mouth to speak and added, 'Yes, Gin, even if it *is* in the middle of the night! I'll be

bursting to tell you about the baby. I don't think I could bear to wait until a sensible time to telephone!'

'Good,' said Ginny.

Then Mum and Dad went.

'And you and I are just going to have to wait now, my lovely,' Gran told Ginny. 'It'll probably be several hours before the baby arrives. You could go round to Sophie's to play if you like?'

'Sophie's away for half-term,' answered Ginny. 'And anyway I've got something that I want to do in my bedroom, if that's all right.'

'That's fine,' said Gran. 'I'll do some baking in the kitchen. I don't want to be too far from the telephone in case there's any news.' Gran did a little dance with her feet. 'Oh, I do wonder what this baby will be like!'

'So do I!'

Chapter Three
WAITING

Ginny spent most of the day in her bedroom just holding and warming the egg. She tried to imagine what its chick would be like.

Suddenly the telephone rang downstairs and Ginny was jolted out of her dreamy mood. Could it be news of the baby? She pulled up her shirt. Placing the egg against the warmth of her tummy and tucking the bottom of her shirt back into her waistband, she secured the egg in place. Then, pulling down her baggy jumper to hide the tell-tale bulge, she headed for the stairs.

In the hall Gran had snatched the telephone from the wall without even pausing to wipe the pastry mix from her fingers, but Ginny could see from her face that it wasn't news of the baby.

'Wrong number? No, no, not to worry. Goodbye!'

21

Gran grinned at Ginny as she put the receiver back. 'Look what a mess I've made!' She wiped the receiver with the bottom of her apron. Then she noticed that Ginny was clutching her stomach again, just as she had done in the garden in the morning. 'Have you got a tummy-ache, love?' she asked.

Ginny shook her head but then she saw Gran looking at the hand that was cradling the egg through the layers of clothes. Gran's eyebrows lifted.

'I think I'd better bring down your quilt and make you snug and warm on the sofa,' she said. 'We don't want you going down with anything or you won't be allowed into the hospital to visit Mum and your new brother or sister!'

Ginny let herself be tucked up and accepted a hot drink. It was nice resting under the covers and nursing the egg in warm hidden peace while her mind wondered about the days ahead. How was she going to care for the chick once it had hatched? How long could she keep it secret?

Gran brought Ginny a jam tart straight

from the oven. 'Careful, mind,' she said.
'The jam'll be a lot hotter than the pastry!'
Then she saw the look on Ginny's face and
added, 'You look miles away!'

'Oh, just thinking. You know,' said Ginny.

'Yes, I know,' smiled Gran.

But this time, thought Ginny, Gran didn't
actually know. She felt a bit guilty, keeping
the egg secret from Gran. Gran was special.

Ginny's gran was a small stocky lady, not
much taller than Ginny herself, and her grey
hair was cut short in a no-nonsense style.
Nothing like the curled perms that most
people's grandmothers seemed to have. And
yet Gran was beautiful. Her eyes sparkled
and she moved with the easy grace of

somebody who was always on the move. Her clothes weren't fussy either. They were practical and tough. But the effect was pleasing, especially as she usually wore a brooch or ear-rings that had some tale of her past life associated with them. Today she was wearing the lovely mother-of-pearl brooch that Grandad had given her when Mum was born.

'Gran?' said Ginny. 'Did you wear that brooch on the day that I was born? Are you wearing it for the baby being born today?'

Gran smiled. 'Yes,' she said, and she sat down on the sofa beside Ginny's covered toes. 'Except that you weren't born in the daytime!'

Ginny had heard this story many times before and she loved it. 'Go on,' she said.

'Well,' said Gran. 'Maggie, your mum, went into labour in the early hours of midsummer morning and she and Dad went off to the hospital. Owen, your grandad, and I spent all day with fluttering tummies waiting and wondering about our first ever grandchild. Well, we heard nothing all day and it got later and later. We busied ourselves with all sorts of jobs that didn't take us too far from the telephone. I remember that Owen cleaned out a drain and I made so much strawberry jam that I ran out of jam jars and ended up bottling it in milk bottles because I didn't want to leave the telephone long enough to see if a neighbour could lend me any jars!

'Anyway, by midnight we had run out of jobs and we decided that we really should go to bed. I pinned my mother-of-pearl brooch onto my nightie. I don't know why, really. I just felt that it was a link between me and your mum. Margaret means pearl, you know. That's why Owen had chosen mother-of-pearl for me when Maggie was born. Anyway, Owen was soon snoring asleep but I lay in bed wide awake. I was far too excited to sleep. And then, at last, the telephone rang! Well, I jumped to answer it, but I found that I was stuck! The brooch had tangled with the blanket and I couldn't get free! You can't imagine how I felt, stuck in bed with that telephone ringing down in the hall with the news I had been longing for and your grandad still snoring beside me! My fingers were too excited to work properly and I couldn't untangle the brooch and all the time I was terrified that whoever was telephoning would give up. I shouted at Owen, but he still didn't wake so I did something awful.'

Ginny grinned.

'I picked up a vase of flowers that was on my bedside table and I poured it over your grandad's head to wake him! He was soaked and the bed was soaked and there were bits of wet leaf and flower everywhere, but it didn't matter. It got Owen to the phone and in moments he was calling up to me, "It's a girl! A beautiful little girl and they're all fine." Oh, it was a special moment, that!' Gran gave Ginny a big hug. 'A very special moment.'

'And then you had to tidy up?' asked Ginny. She didn't want the story to end.

'Yes, then your grandad came and untangled me and we danced round the room together! After a while we cleared up the flowery mess in the bed. It didn't properly dry out for weeks after, but it was worth it!'

'And you ate sardines on toast and drank cocoa,' finished Ginny.

'Yes. Quite delicious! And now,' said Gran, brushing jam-tart crumbs off Ginny's quilt, 'if you're in the mood for family stories perhaps we could do a bit of that patchwork together?'

Mum and Ginny had started to make a piece of patchwork when Mum was first pregnant and over the months it had grown to a size almost big enough to make a cot quilt for the baby. All the books said that you should rest when you were pregnant, but Mum was no good at resting. If she tried just sitting or lying on a bed she soon jumped up again, impatient to get on with something, so the patchwork was a good way to make her sit down. Ginny did it with Mum. She enjoyed cutting out the paper hexagons and carefully stitching the fabrics to them. She enjoyed deciding which materials looked nice next to each other and, even more, she loved hearing Mum talk about where each bit of material had come from. Each patch had a story to tell. There were the bold stripy pieces that came from the deckchair cover that had torn and sent Uncle Thomas sprawling on the lawn last summer. There was a bit of the pretty blue dress that Ginny had had new for her seventh birthday party and then spoilt that same day with dandelion stains as she collected food for her new rabbit. There was a bit of Gran's old apron that had at last fallen to bits and a piece of shimmering white silk left over from Mum's wedding dress. There was a checked patch that was a bit of Dad. It came from a blue check shirt of his that had been in a wash that went wrong and turned everything pink.

Ginny looked at the patchwork now. Just a few more patches and it would be ready for the baby's cot.

'We need something for Grandad,' said Ginny. 'There's nothing for him yet.'

'Yes, you're right,' said Gran. 'Will you be all right for a moment if I pop home and see if I can find a scrap of something that will remind us of Grandad?'

So Gran went and fetched a piece of soft brown checked shirt material that was the sort that Grandad had always worn. While Gran was out of the house Ginny checked that the egg was safe. And then she and Gran sewed and talked and glanced at the telephone together until it was evening.

Ginny went to bed early but she didn't sleep. She made a small warm cave for the egg to lie in by propping up her quilt with one arm. The light on her bedside table dimly lit the dark space and Ginny lay beside the egg and watched and waited.

Chapter Four
HELLO, EGG!

Hours passed and Ginny heard Gran go to bed. The light from the landing went out, and soon after that the egg rocked slightly from side to side and new muffled scratching sounds joined the soft thumps.

Suddenly Ginny breathed in sharply as a hair-thin line of a crack appeared and grew across the smooth surface of the egg. It ran zig-zagging around the waist of the egg, breaking the perfect wholeness, but promising that soon Ginny would see her chick. Her breathing quickened with excitement. The crack spread like a fast-drawn black line, and then the egg lay still for a moment or two as though whatever was inside it had exhausted itself with the effort of cracking the shell. Ginny reached out a finger, wanting to stroke the shell, and she whispered, 'Come on, little one. You're nearly out!' But as her finger touched it, the shell suddenly jolted apart into two golden cupped halves. Lying crumpled between the pieces of shell was something tiny and breathing and damp and greeny-grey.

'A frog!' squeaked Ginny, but as she said it she knew that was nonsense. Frogs came from tadpoles that came from little jelly eggs. Then what? Perhaps some kind of lizard?

Ginny watched, entranced, as the little creature slowly uncurled and revealed itself, pulling itself free of the sticky egginess that had stuck it down in an oval huddle and

dulled the colours of its body. She watched as the head and neck uncurled. The head had large nostrils and surprising lines of dark lashes on either side marking where the eyes were. But the eyes themselves stayed closed. As the unseeing head rose on its long neck, the little body lurched back, and wobbly short scaly legs uncurled and propped up its front half. Another lurch and the back legs were up and a miniature dragon stood for a moment before it crumpled down again onto the sheet. Two more faltering tries, and then he stood firm.

'Hello, Egg!' whispered Ginny, and the dragon's head tipped to one side, trying to work out where the sound of her voice was coming from.

'I'll clean you up, little dragon, and then you'll be able to see.'

Ginny gently pushed back her quilt and stepped out of bed. She tiptoed quietly along the landing to the bathroom and then carried back a tooth mug full of warm water. She took a box of paper tissues from on top of her chest of drawers and knelt beside the bed where the little dragon lay.

In the soft dim light of her bedside lamp, Ginny carefully dampened a corner of tissue and reached across to wipe the eggy stuff that covered the dragon's face. She wiped on down the ridged scaley back to reveal the glowing greeny-blue, purpley-grey shimmering magical colours that lay beneath the stickiness.

'Oh, Egg, you're beautiful! Now, don't be frightened. I'm going to lift you onto my lap so that I can wipe properly around your eyes.'

Ginny cupped her hand under the warm damp little body and lifted. The tiny dragon had a surprisingly solid feel to it, but soft too. Ginny could feel the delicate throb of a

heartbeat against the palm of her hand. From head to tail the dragon was no longer than the length of the hand he sat on. Ginny gently took the head between two fingertips and dampened a fresh corner of tissue. Then, very carefully, she wiped over the dark lashes, one side and then the other. When the eggy gunge had been cleaned away the little dragon's eyes eased open. They opened slowly and jerkily, as if even the soft slight light from the lamp was too bright for eyes that had never seen any light before. They were big eyes for that size of head. They were dark and deep and round. The eyes blinked and then they looked at Ginny in a puzzled, unfocused way.

'Can you see me now?' she asked, a little uncertainly. Egg blinked a slow blink of both eyes together. When they opened again they looked at Ginny and she smiled back. Ginny washed the rest of the wrinkly little face and then on down the rest of the soft skin of the neck and belly. By the time she had finished the soft underside of the legs, the skin on the dragon's face had dried to a soft smoothness like chamois leather. The wrinkled crumpled too-long-in-the-bath look had gone, and the little beast looked more solid. He also looked tired. Ginny smiled as the stumpy green legs suddenly folded down onto the sheet, the eyelashes closed down onto green cheeks again, and the little dragon fell asleep. 'Worn out by being born, are you?' whispered Ginny, and she stroked the tiny soft flat top of his head.

Ginny herself didn't feel at all sleepy. It was past one o'clock in the morning and everything was dark and quiet, but Ginny had never felt less like sleeping. She threw away the used tissues and climbed back into bed. She pulled the quilt over herself and over the tiny dragon beside her. Now that he was curled up again in sleep, Ginny could cave the whole of him under one cupped hand. What was she going to do with him? For the moment she was content with his just being there.

Chapter Five
THE BABY!

It may have been hours or it may have been minutes that Ginny stayed like that. But suddenly the shrill sound of the telephone rang urgently downstairs.

'The baby!'

Ginny leapt out of bed and galloped down the stairs behind Gran. It was surprising how fast Gran ran down the stairs and twirled around the newel post at the bottom. She snatched up the telephone receiver, her face pink and eager and Ginny hopped up and down beside her. The one-sided conversation from Gran's end puzzled her.

'Stephen? It is Stephen, isn't it? Yes, you sounded a bit strange, that's all. No, never mind that. Tell me! Tell me about the baby, for goodness sake!'

And then there was a long gap when Gran didn't say anything, but Ginny watched her

face. It sagged from excited pink to a dull grey. Gran clutched the receiver with two hands now. She propped herself for support against the hall table.

'What is it, Gran? What is it?' Ginny asked.

But Gran just laid a restraining hand on Ginny's shoulder and went on talking to Dad. 'Oh, Stephen! Of course it's a shock, but it'll be all right, I promise you. And Maggie, how's my Maggie?

'Give yourselves time, love. It's very early days. You can't expect to know how you really feel straight away.' Then Gran looked at last at Ginny and said, 'Now, Stephen, I've got Ginny here, impatient for news.'

'Let me talk to Dad!' implored Ginny, but

Gran turned her telephone ear away from Ginny and she listened to Dad again before going on.

'Yes – yes – I'll tell her. Not tomorrow. No, OK. No, don't you worry about us. So we'll see you in an hour or so's time? Yes, of course. No, I quite understand. Lots of love to Maggie and, and to – has he got a name yet?'

Ginny was jumping up and down. 'He! You said he! It's a boy!'

So there is a baby and he is alive! Ginny felt as though her heart was safe to start beating again now. For an awful, dry-mouthed couple of minutes she had begun to wonder.

Gran put down the phone and then hugged Ginny hard. 'You've got a baby brother!' she said in a too-jolly voice. 'He weighs just over six pounds and he hasn't got a name yet.'

'But Mum, is Mum all right?' asked Ginny.

'Yes, Mum's fine.' But Gran still wasn't properly looking at her. She wouldn't meet Ginny's eyes with her own.

'Then what's wrong with the baby?

Something's wrong, isn't it? Tell me, Gran!' and Ginny shook Gran's arm as if she thought she could shake the information out of her.

'Well,' admitted Gran, 'yes, there is a problem. But Dad wants to tell you about it himself when he comes home. Don't worry, love. It isn't that bad!'

As Ginny followed Gran up the stairs Gran pulled herself slowly up, one step at a time. She looked old.

Back in her bedroom Ginny reached out for the sleeping tiny bundle of dragon. She held Egg close to her chest and curled herself round him in an egg-shaped huddle under the covers. 'Oh, Egg,' she said. 'Something's wrong with our baby and they won't tell me what!'

Chapter Six
WHAT DO YOU WANT?

Ginny woke from one of those deep dreams that twists to fit the real world. She dreamt that her bed was coming alive and moving under her but woke to find that what was moving under her hand was the little dragon waking from his own dreams.

Ginny stroked down Egg's rough warm back and Egg opened his eyes. 'Hello, funny face.'

Egg focused his dark deep eyes on Ginny's and blinked a slow smiling blink of hello. He stood himself up, a bit unsteadily, and then his tiny jaw dropped open to stretch into a surprisingly pink yawn. Ginny laughed, but stopped laughing as the yawn suddenly turned into a loud squeal.

'Shush, you silly thing!' She put her finger to her lips in urgent sign language even though she knew that the gesture would mean nothing to the dragon. Egg tipped back his head, opened his mouth again and squealed even louder. It was a piercing, demanding noise, and Ginny instinctively clapped her hand tight over him like a lid.

'Gran might hear!' she whispered. 'Shush!' Under her hand the squeal came again and she could feel tiny tickling leathery paw pads scrabbling at her hand in an attempt to escape.

'What do you want?' asked Ginny, and she lifted his head with a finger so that she could

see his face. She didn't expect the little dragon to answer but he did. He opened his mouth and squealed again, louder than ever. She must do something to stop that noise! Without really thinking about it, Ginny sat up in bed and, with Egg in her hands, she gently rocked him to and fro. As she cradled and rocked, Egg sank down on his side, his eyes drooped and his mouth closed. Now that he was quiet Ginny could think, and it was suddenly obvious what Egg had been squealing about.

'You're hungry, aren't you!' she said. 'You stay up here and be quiet and I'll get dressed and find you some food.' But the moment she put Egg down, his eyes and mouth opened and the squeals started again. Ginny scooped him into her hands and rocked them hard. She could hear Gran moving about in the bedroom next to hers.

'I'm trying to do what you want, you silly thing!' she told him. 'I can't keep rocking you and get food at the same time, can I! Which do you want?' She held the dragon up to her face and looked into his eyes. Egg

42

squealed a long wobbling, ear-hurting squeal and a moment later there was Gran's voice outside Ginny's door.

'Are you all right in there, Gin?'

'Yes, Gran.' Ginny tried to sound unflustered. 'I just turned my tape recorder on too loudly.' Still rocking Egg in her left hand, she put a cassette into her tape recorder and pushed the 'On' button with her right.

Egg put his head on one side, shut his mouth and listened as the music started. Its rhythmic beat seemed to have the same effect on him that rocking had. Gradually Ginny slowed her rocking hand, and then stopped.

Egg whimpered, but he didn't squeal again. She reached for her half-empty handkerchief box and gently laid the dragon down onto the soft white tissues. The cardboard sides of the box hid Egg. His mouth stayed shut and he snored softly. Ginny grabbed her dressing gown from the back of the door and pulled it on. 'I'll be back soon,' she whispered and then headed quickly for the stairs.

What would a baby dragon eat? He must have eaten egg when he was inside the egg. That was what happened, wasn't it? Baby birds inside eggs must eat the yolk and white of the egg or there wouldn't be room for them as they grew! But as Ginny opened the kitchen door, thoughts about Egg and eggs disappeared.

'Dad! You're home!'

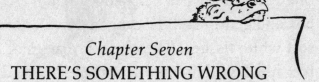

Chapter Seven
THERE'S SOMETHING WRONG

Gran was by the window, cutting bread for toast. Dad was sitting at the table and cradling a mug of coffee in his hands. He looked pale and tired.

'Are you OK?' Ginny asked. She hadn't thought about the baby or Mum and Dad since waking up. Ginny stood behind Dad's chair and wrapped her arms around his neck. She kissed his rough, unshaven cheek and Dad patted her hands.

'Yes, love. A bit shaken up, but I'm OK.' Then he took a deep breath. 'Ginny,' he said and he pulled her round to face him. 'Ginny, love, our baby has something wrong with him. He has Down's syndrome. Something went wrong when he was being made, and he'll – well – he'll always be a bit different. He looks different from other babies and he will always be a bit slow at learning how to do

things. And,' Dad pushed a hand through his hair, 'oh, it's so hard to explain!'

'Do you mean that he's mentally handicapped?' asked Ginny.

Dad looked her properly in the face now. 'Yes, that's it!' he said, relieved that he wouldn't have to struggle to explain more. 'I didn't know that you knew about things like that!'

'Yes, of course I do! And we've got a boy with Down's syndrome at school in the Infants. Mark Naylor. You know, Ben's brother.'

'Oh!' Dad was surprised. 'Well, anyway, we don't know how bad the handicap is yet, but the doctors say that he seems to be quite a healthy baby. Perhaps he might go to your school some day!' Dad did a real smile at last and picked up his mug and sipped the coffee. 'Euch!' he said, and spat it out again. 'I think I'd better make a fresh cup!'

'Let me do it,' said Gran, 'and I'll get you something to eat too.'

Ginny poked Dad in the ribs to get his attention. 'What are we going to call him?' she asked. 'And when can I see him and Mum?'

Dad sagged into his chair again. 'We haven't picked a name yet, love. And Mum doesn't feel ready for visitors.'

'But I'm not visitors!' said Ginny. 'I'm *me*!'

'Oh, Ginny, of course you're not ordinary visitors but Mum really can't face seeing anyone just at the moment.' Dad paused. 'We weren't expecting any problems with the baby you see, Gin.' He looked at her, willing her to understand.

Ginny frowned and Dad tried again. 'All those jokes that we made about the baby

47

playing football for England when he kicked inside Mum – well, we didn't really think that he would play for England. But we did think that he would learn to walk and talk, grow up, get a job, have children, all those usual sort of things. And now some of those things might never happen. It takes getting used to.'

'But he's still my brother! My brother as well as your baby! And your grandson, Gran. Don't you want to see him?'

Gran nodded. 'Yes, of course I do, love. But if Mum isn't ready to see us yet, then it won't do us any harm to wait a day or two until she is. She needs time to work out her own feelings about the baby before she can cope with other people.'

It still didn't make any sense to Ginny though. Having Mum and the baby shut away was wrong! 'But . . .' she started to protest.

'Just leave it for now, Ginny,' warned Gran. 'We need to persuade your dad to go and get some sleep before he goes back to the hospital. Mum's having a rest now – they gave her some pills to help her sleep – but poor Dad hasn't slept since the night before last.'

'What about the baby then?' asked Ginny. She was getting angry now. 'If Mum's asleep and Dad isn't there, then who is looking after him?'

'The nurses are doing that,' soothed Gran. 'He's in very good hands. Newborn babies are asleep most of the time.'

'But he's only less than a day old! He should be with one of us!'

Dad sighed and got up wearily from the table. 'I'll go to bed,' he said.

Ginny got up to. She banged her chair into the table, her temper rising. 'But I could be with him! Or you could, Gran! You know about looking after babies!'

Gran stroked a soothing hand over Ginny's head. 'Don't keep going on, chick. You've got to try and understand.'

But how could she understand? They had all of them – Mum, Dad, Gran and her – longed for this baby for years. Now at last he was here and they wanted to behave as

though he wasn't! Ginny pushed the unbrushed tangle of her hair out of her eyes and was about to try again to make *them* understand when she suddenly remembered Egg upstairs in the tissue box.

'Um,' she ducked her head so that the hair flopped back over to hide her face, 'can I have an egg for breakfast please?'

Gran nodded and turned to the egg rack, glad that the subject of the baby seemed to have been dropped.

'I'll take a drink upstairs to have while I get dressed,' said Ginny, pouring herself a cup of milk. Then, as Gran looked a bit doubtful, 'Mum lets me do it.'

'Oh, go on then,' said Gran. 'Everything's so much at sixes and sevens today that I don't suppose it matters. Mind you don't spill it on your carpet, though.'

'I won't,' Ginny promised and then she hurried back up the stairs.

In her bedroom the tape was just ending and the little dragon was starting to stir awake in his tissue-box bed. As Ginny stripped off her pyjamas and pulled on knickers, shirt, jeans and a jumper, Egg's bright dark eyes opened. Ginny looked down and as he saw her there he slow-blinked a hello. Ginny put her hand into the box and carefully lifted him out. She cradled his warm body in one hand and covered it with the other like a blanket, leaving his head sticking out of one end and his stumpy green tail curling out of the other. She rocked him and spoke soothingly as she pushed and wriggled her sockless feet into slippers.

Egg opened his pink mouth and squeaked quite gently in an up-and-down way. He tipped back his head and did one of his loud squeals. Ginny looked nervously towards the door.

'Shush! Yes, I do understand that noise

51

and I've brought you some milk!' she said
and let him sniff the cup of milk to show him
what she meant. His tiny tongue flickered
out and in. Ginny sat on her bed and watched
him drink.

She thought of Mum sitting in a hospital
bed, all alone. Mum would be hating it. She
was what Dad called 'a very impatient
patient' and now she was stuck in hospital
and unhappy. Perhaps Ginny could send her
some of the patchwork quilt to work on?
Ginny wished she could talk to Mum to cheer
her up. At least she could write to her.

Ginny reached for her pens and paper.
Mum had once told her that green was a
soothing colour. Ginny took the light and
dark green pens and made a border of green

stripes around the paper. Then she looked at the dark blue, the black and the brown and decided that those colours looked too gloomy. She put them on one side. She wanted to cheer Mum up so she took the orange, red, light blue and pink to do each letter in turn and wrote —

Dear Mum,
Please let me come and see you. I want to meet our baby.
Here is some quilt for you to do.
    Your loving Ginny

P.S. I think that you should only sew the bottom half of each patch.

The P.S. was because Ginny remembered visiting a clock shop where Dad had pointed out how every clock and watch had been stopped at ten to two.

'Because it looks like smiles on the clock faces,' he said. 'It makes the shop seem a happy place and makes you more inclined to buy.'

Ginny thought that if Mum sewed the bottom part of the hexagons, then they too would look like a smile and might help make her happier.

Ginny put everything together and wrote 'For Mum' on the bag and left it outside Mum and Dad's bedroom door where Dad was bound to trip over it when he came out. Then she took a deep breath and returned to her room.

Egg was rolling on his back on the floor fighting with Ginny's prickly hairbrush.

'You're as daft as that brush is!' she told him, and she tickled his tummy with the tip of a finger.

Chapter Eight
SO STRANGE, SO NEW

Egg liked the boiled egg. Ginny fed him little bits of it on the tip of her finger and felt the tickle of his tongue as he licked it off. He drank some more milk too, this time from the egg cup. Ginny watched him drink with his feet braced apart to hold himself steady. Egg was filling up with food and drink and he had stopped squealing, but Ginny still felt that he needed something else. He didn't look happy. She curved a hand over his back and hoped that it made him feel safe and warm.

Ginny was still puzzling in her mind what it was that Egg needed and she didn't notice the window cleaner until it was too late to hide Egg. The window cleaner suddenly popped his head up on the other side of the glass and started waving at Egg with a grubby rag. Egg jumped and stretched and pounced after the rag and the window cleaner's eyes opened wide and his mouth dropped open. He tested Egg, stopping the rag still and then suddenly wiping across to the other side of the window. Left and right, up and down, Egg followed, his tail thrashing, a grin on his face and his colours glowing. The window cleaner looked through the glass at Ginny as she sat on her bed, not knowing what to do.

'How d'you do that?' he asked. Ginny

cupped a hand behind one ear and pretended that she couldn't hear.

When Dad was paying him later Ginny heard the window cleaner say something about 'the toys that children have these days', but luckily Dad wasn't really listening.

Seeing Egg playing at the window gave Ginny an idea. She put him on her dressing table in front of the mirror and waited to see what he would do when he saw himself there. As soon as he saw the little dragon in the mirror Egg squealed an excited high-up squeal before he remembered his manners, stood back and slow-blinked a polite hello. The other dragon seemed to blink a hello back and Egg jumped up and squealed again. Ginny laughed as Egg tried to reach through the mirror and touch his new friend. With his scale colours suddenly gleaming more brightly than Ginny had seen them before, Egg stood up on his stumpy little back legs and scrabbled his paws on the mirror, trying to climb in. As he clawed at the glass Ginny suddenly noticed the desperate keenness in Egg's eyes. It wasn't just a game.

'Do you think that's your brother?' she asked him. 'Or a friend?'

Egg didn't answer. He went on bumping his little snout onto the cold hard glass until Ginny gently pulled him away. 'It's only a reflection,' she told him. 'Not real life.'

Egg warbled then, his up-and-down questioning warble and waited, head on one side, for Ginny to answer, but she couldn't.

'I don't understand,' she told him, 'I don't know what you want.' She stroked soothingly down his spine and offered him some more milk in the egg cup. The thought that she couldn't quite work out started creeping around in her mind again.

At suppertime Dad gave Ginny a note from Mum. All it said was –

My Ginny,
Please come and see me tomorrow.
Will you?
   I love you,
      Mum
         x x x

'Brilliant!' she said and hugged Dad hard. 'Can we go first thing?' Dad nodded and kissed the top of her head.

It worried her, though. What would she do with Egg when it was time to go to the hospital?

At three o'clock the next morning Egg squealed. Ginny stumbled out of bed to feed him and noticed something that jolted her awake.

'You've grown!' she said, making Egg jump with her sudden exclamation. 'You weren't that size last night!' Egg put his head on one side, worried by the accusing tone of her voice. 'Oh, it's not your fault!' she assured him and she picked him up and held him to her cheek. Egg snuffled into her ear, nosing through her tangle of hair and tickling her. She had to hold up both hands for his feet to stand on now.

'No wonder you're a hungry dragon,' she told him. 'You're twice the size you were.' And if he could grow that much in one day, then how big would he grow in a week? How big would he grow before he stopped growing?

Ginny lifted Egg up and down and then added in a puzzled voice, 'But you're not any heavier.' That was odd. Ginny stroked gently down his bright smooth scales. As her fingers worked down his back she felt small bumps on his shoulders that she hadn't noticed before. Egg looked up at her and his colours glowed brightly for a moment in the dark.

'Are you growing wings, my little Egg?' she asked and then added, 'You're growing up.'

Egg half-closed his eyes and began to sing. It was the most beautiful sound that Ginny had ever heard. It was like the noise that you make if you run a wet finger around the rim of a wine glass – high and ringing and it came and went and buffeted like a breeze. Part of her wanted him to go on and on with the beautiful song, but part of her was alarmed. It was so strange, so new. The song soared and dipped and rose and spun.

'A flying song,' she spoke in wonder. 'You're going to fly! Lucky you!' He would leave her on the ground when he did.

Ginny leaned back on her pillow as her

head fizzed with questions that needed urgent answers. How big would Egg grow? What sort of creature would he turn into? How could she keep him safe and secret? She knew that she wasn't going to be able to sleep until she had some answers so, with Egg tucked under the flap of her dressing gown, Ginny crept quietly down the stairs and into the sitting room.

The sudden brightness when she switched on the light made both Ginny and Egg blink. She put Egg onto the floor and he buried his face in the hem of a long curtain to shield his eyes from the light. Then he held the curtain between his paws and peeped one bright dark eye round and squealed, willing Ginny to join him in a game of peepo, but she wanted to find her answers.

'Just play quietly,' she told him and then she turned to the bookshelves.

There wasn't a book about dragons so Ginny took out the dictionary and looked up the word 'dragon'. The dictionary told her that dragons were: 'Mythical monsters, part serpent, part crocodile, with strong claws and

scaly skin, generally represented with wings and sometimes breathing out fire.' Ginny chewed the inside of her cheek. That description sounded like some sort of monster. She read on. It said that dragons 'often guarded great treasure'. But what 'great treasure' could little Egg possibly have to do with? Ginny wondered. And the book had got it wrong if 'mythical' meant that dragons didn't really exist. If the book had that bit wrong, then the rest was probably wrong too!

'Look!' Ginny told the dictionary. 'There he is! He's a real dragon!' and she pointed it towards where Egg had been. But he wasn't there now. For a long horrible moment Ginny just stood, her insides frozen. Could the dictionary be right after all?

But then she saw him. Egg was swinging from the curtain tie-back half-way up the wall. He was chewing at its tassel. Bits of tassel fell to the floor in a real mess. Ginny breathed out. Egg was real.

'You're a bad lad!' she told him. 'Don't you dare chew at the one that shows!' As long as he only chewed the tassel that was hidden by the sofa, it wouldn't matter too much and Ginny was so glad to see Egg that she couldn't make herself very cross with him.

After 'dragon', the dictionary had a bit about the word 'dragonet'.

'Are you a dragonet, Egg?' Ginny asked him. It sounded promising, as if it should mean a baby dragon. But it didn't, a dragonet was only a 'brightly coloured spiny fish'. So that was no help.

Egg was squeaking at some new game and trying to catch Ginny's attention. He was behind the sofa and she couldn't see him, but Ginny resisted the temptation to look. She must find out more. Pushing her hair out of her eyes, Ginny went on reading. 'Dragoon' came next. That was getting further away from dragon but what it said was interesting. Dragoons were soldiers named after the sort of guns they used. The guns were called dragons because when they were fired, flames came out of their muzzles. Ginny chewed at the inside of her cheek again. Guns were fired in order to kill. And dragons in stories killed! What about St George and the dragon?

Bang! Something exploded behind the sofa. Ginny jumped, her heart beating fast.

Chapter Nine
YOU WANT YOUR MUM

'Egg! What have you done?'

A small green nose poked round the side of the sofa. Two dark eyes followed and then all the rest of Egg crept out. His eyes were open wide in round deep circles of alarm. Egg saw Ginny and he ran clumsily over to her and buried his nose in her dressing gown. Ginny reached down and picked him up.

Egg had chewed at the long flex that ran behind the sofa from a socket to a tall standing lamp. He had pulled the whole lamp over and the bulb had exploded. Hundreds of sharp slithers of glass were scattered on the carpet.

'You could have been electrocuted!' she told him and hugged him tight. Egg blinked sleepily. 'Time to get back to bed,' she said.

Ginny quickly swept the broken glass into a dustpan and then tidied the bits of chewed tassel out of sight. She closed the dictionary. 'Stupid book,' she told it. 'It was *men* who fired the guns. It was *people* doing the killing. You can't blame the guns for that!' She looked at Egg as he lay snoozing in an armchair. 'And you shouldn't blame dragons either! It's not fair to call a horrible thing like a gun after anything except the men who make them and use them.'

Then Ginny opened the book up again, just so that she could really slam it shut.

'Anyway, what about dragonflies? What about snapdragon flowers?' she asked it. 'They are both beautiful things that wouldn't and couldn't hurt anything. Stupid book!' And she shoved it into its place on the shelf. She noticed that the dictionary's posh blue spine was only fake leather and she found that comforting. 'Nothing about you is true!' she told it.

Ginny went back to bed but she couldn't sleep. Every time she closed her eyes and tried to sleep she imagined Egg turning into the dictionary monster dragon. She saw him breathing out fire like a gun and she had to open her eyes again fast and look at little Egg, soft and kitten-sized, as he lay curled up beside her. It reminded Ginny of the nightmares about tigers under the bed that she used to have when she was little. Then Mum had always made things better. She wished very much that she could creep into Mum and Dad's bedroom now. She wanted to snuggle next to Mum and be told not to worry, but she couldn't. Mum was in the hospital on the other side of town.

Ginny looked down at Egg as he snored beside her and she suddenly knew what it was that was making his colours dull.

'You want *your* mum, too, don't you?' she whispered. 'You want your *real* mum! Not me!'

Egg snored on, but Ginny knew that she had found the thought that had been tickling in her mind all day and that she hadn't dared to think. Egg had a dragon mother – or else who had laid his egg? But why had she laid it in the hen house? Why not wherever dragons live? Ginny sat up in bed. Would the dragon mother be looking for Egg, wanting him

back? Would she be like the monster dragon of Ginny's nightmare? Ginny's heart was beating so fast and hard that it seemed to be jumping around right up in her throat.

'Egg, she'll think that I've stolen you!' she said. 'She'll come to get you back!' Ginny glanced towards her window. Her curtains hung limp and calm as normal and even though Ginny scrunched up her face and strained her ears until they felt the size of satellite dishes on either side of her head, she couldn't hear any unusual noises from outside. But she daren't get out of bed and actually look. Ginny's alarmed voice had risen above a whisper and Egg's eyes blinked awake. She was glad.

'What's she like?' she asked. 'Egg, could

you *hear* how big she was from inside your shell?' Egg rested his head on Ginny's chest and gazed up at her. 'I'm sure that your mum will come for you,' she assured him. 'I would if I was her. And we need a plan ready for when she does.' And then a thought struck Ginny that filled her with relief. 'But she won't come *here*, will she? She'll go to the hen house where she left you! That's it! I'll put you back in the hen house with the hens! They know all about looking after babies that come out of eggs – that's probably why your mother left you there! And she will come and fetch you from there, I'm sure she will!'

Ginny tried to reassure her thumping heart. Egg could be happy again. And she could be out of danger! *And* she could visit Mum and the baby tomorrow without worrying about Egg. Perfect!

Chapter Ten
YOU'RE GOING HOME

Ginny was up and dressed before it was light. Her body ached with tiredness and pulled her back towards the rest and warmth of bed, but she knew that Egg must be moved now, before Dad or Gran were up.

'Come on, Egg,' she told the sleepy dragon. 'You're going home.'

As she opened the back door and stepped outside, the cold morning air turned her breath into plumes of steam like a real dragon's. Egg was a warm wriggling bundle zipped into her jacket and held firmly under her right elbow.

'You stay there,' she told him as he struggled to get his head out and see. 'You've got to stay hidden in case we meet anyone.' That was part of it, but it also helped Ginny not to have to look into his trusting eyes and know that she was about to leave him.

Ginny hardly recognised her own road as she walked up towards Gran's house. The orange street lamps lit front gardens and the cars parked along the road with a strange light that somehow took away all the colours. Everything looked a bit like an old black and white film, a bit unreal. The curtained windows down the street had a look of eyes closed in sleep. An upstairs light in one house winked brightly into the gloom, but otherwise everything was still and it felt to Ginny as though she was walking in a magical land past rows of sleeping giants.

There were no sounds except the whine of

a milk float in a neighbouring street and a distant swishing of wind in the trees. Ginny could hear her own footsteps in a way that she had never noticed before. If the great dragon mother was out looking for her, then her sound and movement would make her easy to spot. Ginny glanced around.

Suddenly close by came a great flapping sound of huge wings. Ginny froze still on the pavement. She clenched Egg so hard that he squealed. Where was the dragon? It must be hiding near by. Should she drop Egg and run? Hide with Egg? Or stand where she was and face his mother? Oh, but where could she hide?

Then she saw it.

There was no monster. A big grey tarpaulin sheet that was covering the caravan in the front garden next door to Gran's had suddenly flapped in the wind!

Ginny walked fast towards the hen run and talked to the warm wriggling bundle under her arm. 'It'll be nice having all those hens to look after you,' she told Egg. 'Like having six mothers!'

Her mouth talked confidently on but her thoughts went off in a different direction. What about all those eggs that each one of Gran's hens had laid but never had the chance to hatch out? Ginny couldn't remember ever seeing them looking unhappy when their eggs were taken. Did they care?

'Your dragon mother must have meant the hens to look after you or she wouldn't have left you there, would she?' her mouth went on.

Egg wriggled and Ginny clamped him a bit more firmly under her arm.

The hen run looked cold and bleak with its bare earth and wire fence. It would be a bit different from the warm cosy bedroom that Egg was used to.

'Still,' she told him as she unzipped her jacket and pulled him out, 'the hens will keep you warm with their feathers. They might even speak the same language as you and understand your questions!' She looked at him and smiled encouragingly. When Egg slow-blinked trustingly back at her she nearly pushed him back into her jacket and ran home. The scrabbling and clucking noises that were coming from the hungry hens didn't sound anything like beautiful singing dragon language. Could she, should she, leave him?

Ginny thought of Egg's mother and wavered. Then she suddenly remembered that she could visit her new brother in hospital today, and she didn't waver any more. She pulled open the hen-house door and waded her way through the flurry of indignant hens.

'Here you are, Egg,' she said brightly. 'Back where you came from.'

She put Egg down on the dusty dirty floor and busied herself with dealing with the hens' food and water. Would Egg share those

musty hard pellets? In the shadowy, murky morning light he looked small and strange even though he was the size of the hens now. His big dark eyes looked so trusting beside the sharp little eyes of the hens. 'You should be with flying creatures,' she told him.

He looked at her.

'You'll be happy here,' she said.

Still he looked.

Ginny turned and went but his look tugged at her back all the way down Gran's garden, all the way down the road and home. 'I should be feeling free!' she told herself, but the sick feeling of worry remained and a new thought struck her. 'Gran will see him with the hens! Stupid girl! I'll have to tell her now!'

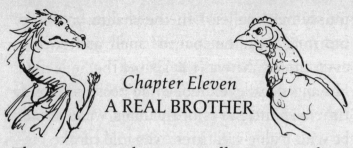

Chapter Eleven
A REAL BROTHER

There was no chance to talk to Gran alone that morning. As soon as breakfast was over Ginny and Dad drove across town to the hospital.

The hospital was big and had a funny bathroom sort of smell to it. Dad knew his way along corridors and past lots of doors until they came to the maternity ward.

'Which room is Mum in?' asked Ginny, her stomach fluttering.

'She's over here,' said Dad and he pointed to a closed door. Dad knocked on the door and waited.

'It's only Mum!' said Ginny. 'Why are you knocking?'

Mum was in a room all on her own. There were no other mothers and, Ginny suddenly realised, no baby!

'Where is he?' she asked. Her hands went

up to her cheeks as if she needed to hold her head steady while her mind spun with awful possibilities. 'Where is he, Mum?'

Mum was pale and the white hospital covers of the bed and the white-painted walls made her seem paler still. Her eyes looked like big dark panda eyes in her white face. The only bright thing in the room was the little pile of untouched patchwork fabrics on the bedside table.

'Ginny, love! Come here!' Mum's voice sounded a bit wobbly. Ginny hugged Mum

and Mum felt strangely different without the baby bump to cushion her front.

'Where's the baby, Mum?' Ginny asked again. 'The other mothers have all got their babies with them. Where's ours?'

Mum held Ginny away from her and looked into her daughter's eager, frightened face.

'Do you really want to see him? Has Dad told you?'

'About him having Down's syndrome? Yes. And *of course* I do!' Ginny stamped her foot as she said it.

'It's just,' Mum looked away from Ginny now, 'it's just that he looks different from other babies, you see. He *looks* like a baby with Down's syndrome. Not like you did, Ginny. Not like, well, like *my* baby.' Mum's mouth began to quiver and Dad put his arm around her. Mum took a deep breath. 'He's in the nursery, Gin. One of the nurses is giving him a feed. Dad can take you along there.'

Ginny took Dad's hand and dragged him through the door and across the corridor to the nursery. A young nurse sat in there with a white bundle on her lap. The baby in the bundle had lots of spiky dark hair capping a round pink face that was being fed with a small bottle. The nurse looked up and smiled.

'You must be big sister?' she said.

Ginny stroked the silky wet-looking hair on the baby's hot little head while the nurse wiped milky dribbles from his mouth and chin. The baby's eyes were closed slits lined by long dark lashes. Ginny longed to see them open. The nurse stood up and nodded her head towards the chair she had been sitting on. 'Here. You sit down. See if you can get him to take some milk.'

Ginny settled herself firmly back into the chair and cradled her arms ready for the baby. He was surprisingly heavy and solid feeling but still very wobbly as the nurse tipped him into her arms. Gran had said that he was small for a newborn baby, but when Ginny thought that only hours before he had been inside Mum he seemed huge!

Supporting the baby's neck and shoulders with her left arm, Ginny held the bottle in her other hand and touched the teat to his

lips. The baby's pink mouth opened and Ginny was surprised by the pull that sucked it in. She grinned up at the nurse and the nurse smiled back. 'He wouldn't take any more from me!' she said.

The baby drank the whole bottle of milk from Ginny. Ginny handed the bottle back to the nurse and had a good look at her brother. He had a squarish fat-cheeked face of the most beautifully fine soft pale skin. He had slightly almond-shaped blue eyes that opened once his concentration on drinking had finished. He looked quizzically up at Ginny and the movement corrugated his forehead.

'Hello!' Ginny whispered and then she couldn't think of anything else to say.

He has a snub nose. Like mine, thought Ginny. And all that fine black hair. Ginny could see that in some ways the baby did look like Mark at school. But Mark had ginger hair and freckles. The baby felt like a real brother to Ginny. She squeezed him in a gentle hug. So why didn't he feel like her own baby to Mum? 'Can you see me properly?' she asked him. 'I'm your sister!'

The baby's eyes wandered in an unfocused way that didn't really look straight at her. Just like Egg's had been when he was newly hatched, she thought. Ginny wondered how Egg was getting on with the hens. She gazed towards the window and then shook her head. She looked back into her brother's bright blue eyes. They're the colour of sky on picture postcards, she thought. And his hair was the same deep black as Egg's eyes. 'One day soon you'll meet him,' she told her little brother.

'Who's he going to meet?' asked Dad, and Ginny looked up in surprise to see Dad, together with Mum, standing in the doorway and watching her.

'He's beautiful, Mum,' she smiled. 'But he does need a name. Everybody needs a name, and we can't just call him "the baby" all the time.'

That seemed to make Mum shrink back towards the door. 'Oh, no. Not yet, Ginny. There's plenty of time to think about that later.' Mum pulled at her dressing gown, hugging it around herself, even though the hospital was hot. 'Come back to my room now, Gin. Tell me all about home,' said Mum and she went.

Ginny looked up at Dad. 'Can't the baby come with us?'

'Better not,' said Dad softly. 'Give him back to the nurse now.'

At least Dad looked at the baby as he said it, thought Ginny. Mum didn't even do that. The nurse held out her arms to take the baby and Ginny reluctantly handed him back. 'See you soon,' she said and then she turned to follow Mum and Dad.

When Ginny looked back from the

doorway she saw that the nurse had her baby brother propped over her shoulder and was jiggling him up and down and humming a tune. The nurse laughed as the baby belched into her ear. She seemed to be enjoying him. It should be Mum doing that, thought Ginny. And it should have been Mum feeding him too. Feeding him properly with breast milk as she had seen Mum doing with her in photographs. There seemed to be more wrong with Mum than with the baby, she thought.

Chapter Twelve
WHY?

In the car on the way home Ginny asked Dad why. Why wasn't Mum looking after the baby? Why hadn't he got a name yet? Why . . .

'Oh, Ginny, please give it a rest!' said Dad, but then he sighed. 'Look, I'm sorry, love, but it's so hard to explain. You've just got to accept that having a handicapped baby has been a shock, particularly for Mum. We've got a lot of thinking and adjusting to do before we're ready to – well – to decide how we are going to cope, I suppose.'

'He's handicapped and we can't change that, so what is there to think about?' asked Ginny.

'Oh.' Dad swept a hand through his hair. His hair needs a wash, thought Ginny. 'I don't want to talk about it.' His voice was rising again. 'Just stop the endless questions, please. It's nothing for you to worry about.'

A horrible thought suddenly came to her. In spite of what Dad had said she couldn't not ask. 'You wouldn't give him away, would you, Dad? Have him adopted?'

'Ginny, please!' said Dad. 'Just stop it!'

Ginny laid her head against the back of the car seat. She remembered seeing on the television news once about how many handicapped babies there were waiting for families to adopt them. Was that what they had to have time to think about? Were they thinking about giving the baby away? Ginny felt so angry that she wanted to shout

something to shock Dad, to make him feel awful for not bringing the baby and Mum home and making everything normal. But then she remembered Egg. She had handed him over to the hens. Was that any different?

Ginny's thoughts spun and she tried to reason with herself. 'It was for him,' she told herself. 'It was to get him back to his mother!' But perhaps she was just making up excuses? Perhaps she had been wrong to leave him with those scratchy hens? Ginny's hands felt cold and clammy. She hadn't meant either to steal or dump Egg, but she had done both. She closed her eyes and tried to think. She sat in the car, pale and quiet and with her eyes tight shut and she suddenly felt a chilling coldness and darkness sweep over her. She knew what it was. In her mind's eye she saw it all; the dragon mother's vast wings shadowing out the sun as she plummeted down towards the car. At any moment now there would be the ripping rasping noise of great dragon talons piercing the car roof and working up and down, up and down as they opened it up like a tin opener opening a can of beans. The dragon would peel back the roof and pluck Ginny out of her seat. A sudden roar came from outside the car window and Ginny felt heat on her face and saw fiery red through her eyelids.

'No!' She screamed as she opened her eyes and saw grey billowing smoke before something hit her hard on the head.

'What on earth are you playing at?' asked Dad.

A car behind them honked.

'You nearly caused an accident!' Then Dad saw Ginny rubbing her head where it had bumped the back of the seat when he had suddenly braked. 'Are you all right?' he asked more gently.

'Yes,' said Ginny.

She saw now what had happened. A great noisy lorry was driving away from the traffic lights beside them. It must have shaded them from the sunshine as it came alongside and then revved its engines and belched out exhaust as it pulled away. 'You stupid thing!' she told herself silently. 'You imagined it all!'

But had she just imagined Egg as well? She must find out.

'Dad, can you drop me off by Gran's and I'll walk the rest of the way home?'

'Yes, of course,' said Dad.

He'll be glad to be rid of me, thought Ginny.

They drove the rest of the way to Gran's in silence, each buried deep in their own thoughts.

Chapter Thirteen
THE FIRE MONSTER

Ginny hurried along the path down Gran's garden. The sun was shining, the birds were singing and everything should have felt fine, but it didn't. Ginny looked anxiously towards the hen run to see whether Egg was out with the chickens. She was looking for green movement but what caught her eye was the menacing movement of something grey. It was a lazy curl of smoke dawdling out from around the hen-house door.

She ran.

'Egg!' she called as she ran. 'Oh, please, Egg!'

Ginny could see all the chickens fussing and flapping in the run, but Egg wasn't with them. He must still be in the hen-house. In her mind Ginny saw the dry straw bales, the dry planking of the floor, doors and roof, and she knew that any fire in there would soon

take hold.

Ginny couldn't see any flames through the dusty hen house window but the smoke was thick. As she wrenched the door open the smoke came at her and grabbed at her throat, making her cough. For a moment it halted her in the doorway but she knew that Egg must be in there somewhere and she had to go in. With smoke fogging her sight and choking her breath, Ginny put her arms out in front of her and swam them through the smoke as she stepped inside and searched, eyes wide and streaming from the stinging smoke. At first she couldn't even see where the musty grey smoke was coming from. There was so much of it, smothering everything and choking her lungs and mind.

She felt dizzy and sick and knew that she had to breathe some fresh air and think. Putting her head out through the doorway for a quick gulp of air, she pulled back from panicky thoughts.

'Come on! Think sensibly or you waste any chance to save him!'

She put one arm up to muffle her mouth and nose from some of the smoke with her jumper sleeve. 'Where did you put him this morning? Come on!' she bullied herself. Ginny closed her eyes and saw more clearly in her mind than her eyes could manage in the smoky hut. She saw Egg, small Egg, down in a corner on the floor.

Ginny crouched down. The smoke was thinner near the floor. Of course it was! Why hadn't she remembered? She knew perfectly well that smoke rises and gets thickest up at the ceiling! She remembered that in a fire you should stay down low, get out of the building and shut doors behind you. And she was still in the hut, with the door wide open! The air would soon stoke the smoky smouldering mess into real fire. It was

happening already. Ginny suddenly saw one bright spark of orange flame blink on the floor in the corner. It wavered uncertainly for a moment and then puffed up into bold scorching fire. Ginny instinctively put up her hands to shield her face, but just before they covered her eyes she saw in the new light from the fire a small huddled dragon. 'Egg!'

Ginny plunged her hands through the flames, down and up, bringing Egg out of the fire. Clutching him to her, coughing and blinking streaming eyes, she stamped furiously at the flames. They had tried to kill Egg and now she was going to kill them. But, as if it were playing some sort of nightmare game, the fire seemed to enjoy her stamping.

Fire danced around her feet, leaping into new areas of straw and flaming them into the game too.

'Let it win the hut, it doesn't matter as long as Egg is safe!' She must get out of the hut before the whole thing exploded into flame. But for a brief moment she hesitated. What about Gran's hen hut? 'Get out!' she shouted out loud this time. She stumbled out into daylight, gasping for air. The garden hose lay beside the hen hut. Ginny gently placed Egg down on a clump of grass away from the hut and then ran her shaking legs up the garden to turn on the tap outside Gran's back door.

Grabbing the hose, Ginny aimed its shining silver blade of water into the orange heart of the fiery hut as it crackled and flickered and breathed out smoke. She stepped towards the burning heat and felt as though she were going into battle with the terrible dragon monster that she had been dreading. Heat and fear prickled and stabbed at her and she felt that the hut's flaming mouth might crash closed and chew her back

into the fire. Clenching the hose tight between her hands she thrust the spear of water back and forth between the flames and the fire monster sizzled with rage and at last died back to a few steamy breaths. Coughing, shaking, but glad, Ginny stepped back from the steamy smoke into the cool clear garden air and let the hose drop from her limp hands.

'So there!' she said, and she pushed the hair and smoke from her face. The blackened wisps of straw blowing in the slight breeze looked pathetic. Ginny felt a bit like Dorothy in *The Wizard of Oz* when she throws water at the wicked witch and the witch sizzles and dissolves away. Then Egg whimpered and, as surely as the water had quenched the fire, worry about Egg quenched Ginny's feelings of triumph. She crouched down beside the soot-smeared, shivering little dragon, put a finger under his slumped head and lifted his chin up. 'Egg?' she asked.

Egg looked at her. His body was dulled with dirt and pain but his eyes opened wide and glittered as he slow-blinked a loving hello. He opened his mouth and sang a ringing cry of welcome. 'You're glad to see me!' whispered Ginny in disbelief. 'Oh, Egg, why?' She patted him clumsily as tears poured down her face, washing the soot from her eyes. 'It'll be hard work,' she told the grubby green head that rested and hummed happily against her chest. 'I'm going to keep you properly now. At home again.' And Ginny suddenly knew that she didn't dread the dragon mother any more. Perhaps she would never come and Egg could stay with her for ever.

'Come on then, Egg,' she said, wiping grimy tears from her face and standing up. 'Let's go home.'

As she stood again, Ginny suddenly felt

wobbly and sick. Bits of her hurt quite a lot. She felt like dirty jelly and she wasn't sure that she could hold on to Egg without dropping him. She sat down again and rested Egg on her lap while her ears and mind buzzed. Ginny looked at him. His scales were dull beneath the soot. 'My poor Egg!' said Ginny. There was a crusting of dark dried blood down the front of his neck and under his belly.

'On all your soft parts,' she said. 'Those hens! They've been pecking at you, haven't they! And I thought that they would look after you. But who started the fire?' What was it that the dictionary said? Those old guns had been named after dragons.

'It was you, wasn't it,' she said sadly. Egg looked up at her. 'You breathed out fire to frighten away the hens.' Egg blinked. 'And it set fire to the straw. Oh, Egg, you mustn't ever do that again! Not if I'm going to keep you! Now I really will have to talk to Gran about you.'

Chapter Fourteen
THIS IS MY DRAGON

Back home Ginny was glad to see Gran in the kitchen getting lunch. She felt very strange, pushing open the kitchen door and standing there, dirty and smelling of fire and holding a young dragon in her arms. Gran turned at the sound of the door opening and stood and stared.

'Gran, I . . .' Ginny faltered, not knowing where to begin. But the sound of Ginny's voice seemed to bring Gran to her senses and Ginny found herself pulled from the doorstep and pushed into a chair.

'Whatever's happened, Gin? You look awful!'

As Gran filled the kettle for a hot drink and pulled muddy shoes off Ginny's feet Ginny felt something that had been cold and hard and strong inside her begin to melt. When she spoke again her voice wobbled. 'There's been a fire, Gran. In the hen house. I've put it out, but it's a mess.'

'Oh, my poor Ginny,' said Gran. 'I should have guessed!'

'Why?' asked Ginny. 'How could you have guessed?'

Egg stirred in Ginny's arms and snuffled a sooty sneeze. Ginny looked down at Egg, humping round on her lap as he settled down for a rest, as large as a puppy now and very obviously real. She looked up. Gran was watching Egg too, watching with a fond smile twitching at one end of her mouth.

'Gran!' exclaimed Ginny. 'Why don't you say something?'

Gran's mouth smiled at both ends now. She didn't look in the least surprised. Ginny tried again. 'Gran, this is my dragon. He's called Egg.'

'And he's a dear little fellow!' said Gran.

'He's a *dragon*, Gran. A real dragon!'

'Yes, I know, chick. I've met one before.' She smiled at Ginny's astonished expression. 'I had a little dragon of my own hatch out and stay when your grandad died.'

Gran looked away and Ginny knew from her faraway look that she was looking back at memories.

'Do you know, I had forgotten all about her until I realised that you had found a dragon too.' She laughed. 'I remember being very cross with all the extra work she was!' Gran stroked the top of Egg's head and tickled behind his ears. 'I was worn out with nursing your grandad and then he died and I just wanted to shut myself away in the home that he and I had shared. I wanted to nurse the memories that were all that were left of

Owen. I didn't want to bother with anyone or anything else. And then I found that blessed egg! I didn't want it! But there it was, helpless and nobody else to care for it so I kept it warm and watched it hatch and out came a little dragon. Do you know, Ginny, there were moments when I almost put that baby dragon out onto the pavement outside my house in the hope that somebody else would find her and look after her! She exhausted me.' Gran smiled. 'And yet I loved her dearly because she loved me. I cried when my little dragon went. I missed her then.' Gran looked down at Egg.

'What was your dragon called, Gran?' asked Ginny.

'I never called her anything but Dragon, I'm afraid,' said Gran. 'You see, I had no intention of keeping her at first. I wasn't even sure if she was real or if I was just an old woman going a bit loopy after your grandad's death. Anyway, I didn't name her, and by the time I came to love her and want her, Dragon seemed to be stuck with that as her name.'

Ginny thought back to that time after

Grandad's death when Gran had shut herself away in her house and they had hardly seen her for days. Mum had told Ginny that Gran 'needed time to grieve.' And all that time she had been busy with a dragon baby!

'Why didn't you tell anyone?' asked Ginny. 'Why didn't you tell Mum about your dragon? Or me?'

'Well,' said Gran, 'I decided that the dragon was quite enough to cope with without worrying about your poor mum thinking I was going dotty as well. And just when I was beginning to feel strong enough to share Dragon with the rest of you, it was time for her to go.'

'Go? Go where?'

Gran put a hand onto Egg's back and fingered the growing wings. The wing lines reached half-way down Egg's body and Ginny could see leathery folds hidden under them. 'Your Egg is almost ready to go,' said Gran quietly.

'No!' said Ginny. 'He isn't going anywhere. He needs me!'

'Not for much longer,' said Gran.

'But I need him,' said Ginny. 'Where will he go?' she added.

'He will go back to his mother once he can fly,' said Gran.

'But why?' asked Ginny. 'Why do dragon mothers leave their eggs if they want the babies back in the end?'

Gran shrugged. 'I don't know all the answers, Gin. I only know that that is what happened to Dragon. She flew off into a beautiful autumn sunset with her mother.' Gran gazed out of the window. 'It was one of those orange glowing evenings when the sun sits on the horizon looking every bit the great ball of fire that it is. Dragon's mother came to my garden and I knew that my job was over. It was a beautiful and a sad time.' Gran paused. 'I thought that I would never forget it, but I had, you know, until you reminded me just now.'

Ginny saw that Gran's eyes were full of tears. When Gran crinkled her eyes into a smile to cheer Ginny the tears tipped over and down her face. Ginny put an arm around Gran's waist, buried her face in Gran's

comfortable soft stomach and thought.

'Gran, was the mother dragon fierce? Was she big?'

Gran laughed. 'Do you know, Gin, I really can't remember her size, but I'm sure that she can't have been frightening or I would have remembered.'

'How old was Dragon before she went?'

Gran thought for a moment. 'I can't say how many days old she was, but I know that it was when she had learnt to fly. That was when she went.'

So there was some time left. Ginny wondered whether she could stop Egg from ever learning how to fly so that he would stay with her for ever. Gran clipped the wings of her hens to stop them from flying, but Ginny knew that she couldn't do a thing like that to Egg.

'I'll go and clean Egg up,' she told Gran. 'He's so dirty and he's been hurt.'

'And I'll go and see what sort of state that hen house is in.'

Up in the bathroom Ginny found some cotton wool and filled a bowl with warm water. She sat on the closed toilet seat, put a towel across her lap and then put Egg onto the towel. As she carefully bathed the soot away, the damp scales down his back glowed their wonderful green-grey-blue-purple just as pebbles in rock pools show colours that are hidden when they are dry.

Ginny took fresh cotton wool and dabbed at the bloody wounds on Egg's neck and belly. His dark eyes flickered with pain as she touched him but he stayed still and gazed at Ginny. She felt a bit as though she were a dragon too. She had tough armour that could keep her safe from some things, but she knew that she had a soft underbelly. She had been strong through the danger of the fire and yet she hurt now.

'I'm sorry I left you with those hens, Egg.'

She felt very muddled. She knew now from Gran that Egg *would* go back to his dragon mother. It was just what she had hoped for only a few hours ago, so why wasn't she happy? Egg slow-blinked at her and she kissed the top of his head.

That evening Dad brought Mum home from the hospital with him. Ginny hugged her so hard that Mum could hardly breathe and Mum hugged Ginny back just as hard. But they came home without the baby.

'Where is he?' asked Ginny. 'Mum, what have you done with him?'

Mum turned away from Ginny's intent face but Dad held Ginny by the shoulders and told her.

'Don't worry, love. We haven't done anything with him. He's at the hospital and will stay there for a few days. The people at the hospital thought it would be a good idea to leave him for a day or two, just to give

Mum and me some time to sort things out. He's being well cared for.'

'But . . .' began Ginny, and this time Mum spoke.

'Just be patient with us, please, Ginny. It would help if you would leave us to think about things in peace,' and Mum turned her back to Ginny and went inside.

Ginny was stunned. Leave them in peace! She wanted to help Mum and Dad, but not by leaving them alone!

Chapter Fifteen
OH, EGG!

Mum and Dad stayed at home. They said that they were resting and thinking, but it looked to Ginny as if they were just wasting time. Dad was using up his holiday time from work and yet he wasn't doing the garden or decorating the bathroom walls that had been stripped of the old wallpaper months ago. He didn't practise his clarinet ready for the jazz concert. Mum didn't do even one patch for the patchwork quilt and, worst of all, she and Dad didn't visit the baby.

'But we could go, couldn't we, Gran?' asked Ginny. She couldn't bear the thought of the baby all alone in the big hospital. What must he be thinking? She wanted to see and hold him again to reassure herself that her little brother was real even if Mum and Dad seemed to be pretending that he wasn't.

Ginny left Egg sleeping when she and Gran

went to the hospital. 'You can have my cardigan,' she told him and made a nest out of it in a high-sided cardboard box. 'You'll be safe in there,' she assured him. Ginny closed her mind to the memory of the fire in the hen house. That had only been because of the hens. It wouldn't, mustn't, happen here in her bedroom.

The hospital was bustling with visitors carrying bunches of flowers and teddy bears and other presents with pink or blue bows on them. Gran and Ginny hadn't brought anything. There didn't seem much point when the baby still had to wear hospital clothes and was too tiny and sleepy to be interested in toys.

'Here he is, Gran.' Ginny pointed to a plastic crib near the nursery's window. She was pleased that she could recognise him so easily. Some of the other babies looked very like each other. But this one was her brother for sure. His black hair spiked up all around his head and his blue, almond-shaped eyes were open.

'Hello, hedgehog!' whispered Ginny. She

reached a hand into the crib and stroked the silky black hair down one side of his warm head. The baby's mouth opened and reached around towards her hand, his tongue working in and out.

Gran laughed. 'Oh, I remember what that means!' she said. 'He's hungry! I'll find a nurse and ask if he's due for a feed. Perhaps we will be allowed to give him his bottle.'

They spent about an hour with the baby. Ginny and Gran both tried feeding him. He drank some of the milk but kept spitting the

bottle's teat out of his mouth. In the end they gave up trying to get any more into him and Ginny held her little brother hugged to her shoulder as she had seen the nurse do on her last visit. He felt heavy to hold and it made Ginny think about Egg again. Egg was still growing fast but he didn't seem to have got any heavier. Ginny had even begun to wonder whether he was actually getting lighter as he got bigger. The wonderful colours of his scales were certainly getting paler. Perhaps that was because they had to stretch to a bigger area as Egg grew, but Ginny felt that it was partly because Egg wasn't happy. But it was strange. This baby, born on the day that Egg had hatched, was still all baby. His head flopped over and she had to support it with one hand. He felt warm and wriggly and smelt nicely milky. Ginny rocked from one foot to the other and soon the baby slumped into sleep. Gran took him gently from Ginny and laid him back in his crib.

The baby lay curled with his knees up and his legs down in a 'G' shape. His fists were up in front of his mouth. They had tiny white hospital mittens on them to stop him from scratching himself. Ginny thought that they made him look like a miniature boxer.

'We'll take on the world together,' Ginny promised him.

'Time to go home,' said Gran.

Back home, Ginny ran up the stairs.

'Egg!' she called quietly as she opened the bedroom door. 'I'm back!' and she knelt beside the cardboard box.

Egg wasn't there.

'Egg!'

She looked around the room, at her bed, her bookcase, the toy corner. He wasn't anywhere.

'Egg!'

She looked under the bed. There was some fluff and a lost button, but no Egg.

'Egg!'

Then she heard him, heard his singing chime from somewhere ¯high up. 'Oh!' Ginny's hands went to her cheeks.

Egg was sitting on the wardrobe, his tail

hanging down and a look on his face that showed that he thought he was being very clever.

'Oh, Egg, get down!' Then, as Egg wobbled on the edge of the wardrobe, 'No, don't!'

Ginny stood with her arms held out ready to catch him, but Egg didn't need catching. As Ginny watched, he unfurled two wonderful wings and gently flapped them to keep himself balanced and the wings on show.

For a moment Ginny couldn't say anything. She just watched. Egg suddenly launched himself off the wardrobe and, flapping his wings rather clumsily, he began to circle the room.

'Oh, they're beautiful!' Ginny found her voice at last.

The wings shimmered pale grey-green-purple, oil-in-a-puddle colours. They were delicate and strong at the same time and they reminded Ginny of Gran's hands.

As he flew, Egg became more confident and flapped less frantically. He glided and soared. As he swooped under the light that hung in the middle of the ceiling, the colours of his wings shone bright and clear and wonderful. Ginny sat down on the bed. She needed to get out of the way of the flying dragon, but she also suddenly felt too busy in her brain to cope with standing up. Egg swooped down to land on the bed beside her. He folded down the wonderful wings and laid his head against Ginny's chest and hummed gently into her body.

'It's time for you to go, isn't it?' said Ginny.

Chapter Sixteen
KITE

'What's the matter, Gin?' asked Mum the next morning. 'You look worried.'

Gran saved Ginny from having to answer. 'Maggie, why don't you and Stephen go out for a walk this morning? It's a lovely sunny spring day and I'm sure that the fresh air would do you good.'

With a smile and a wink at Ginny, Gran bundled Mum and Dad into boots and coats and almost pushed them out through the front door.

'Are you trying to get rid of us?' asked Mum with a smile.

'Yes!' said Gran very firmly. 'Go and walk up Easter Hill, and don't come back until lunchtime!'

Once Mum and Dad were safely out of the way, Gran turned to Ginny.

'Now then, chicken, you've got a job to

do.'

Ginny pushed her tangled fringe out of her eyes and started to stack the breakfast bowls and plates. 'My turn to wash up?' she asked.

'No,' said Gran. 'I think you know what needs to be done.' She put an arm around Ginny and pointed up at the ceiling. 'He needs his dragon mother now,' she said.

'Yes,' agreed Ginny. 'He's been flying.' Then, 'Gran, will you do it with me? Please?'

'No, sweetheart. You have to do this all by yourself.'

'Where?' asked Ginny.

'Back in my garden where you found him,' said Gran.

Ginny went upstairs and thought of what she had to do. She would have to take Egg up the road to get to Gran's garden, in daytime and with people about. Then she would have to wait for the mother dragon. And then she would have to say goodbye to Egg.

Egg was waiting on Ginny's bed and he slow-blinked when he saw her. She put her arm around his soft tummy. He was so big that she couldn't reach all the way round him

now but his lightness made lifting him easy.
Egg hummed into Ginny's chest while she
thought about how she could carry him to
Gran's garden. She couldn't hide him under
her coat any more. He was just too big.
Ginny stroked along the line of a folded
wing. 'I know!' she said. 'You can fly!' But
then she imagined him rising up into the sky
and flying off the moment he saw his
mother. That would be no good. She wanted
to let him go when she was ready. 'I'll tie you
on to a string and you can pretend to be a
kite!' she said.

Ginny found a long ball of string and tied
one end around Egg's plump body. He

snorted a giggle as she reached under his wings.

'Does it tickle?' she asked, and then, 'Does it hurt, Egg?' She was worried that the thin string would cut into him. Perhaps something tucked under the string to pad it would help?

'Oh, I know!' she said, jumping off the bed and lifting the lid of her old dressing-up box. 'I'll turn you into a Chinese dragon with coloured streamers! If anybody stops me down the road, I'll just tell them that you're my Chinese New Year kite!'

Ginny took out three bright silk scarves that Gran had given her ages ago for playing magicians. 'They'll look lovely when you're flying,' she assured him. 'And I bet they'll feel nice too, streaming out behind you.'

Gran was at the door to say goodbye. She patted Egg gently on the head. 'Send love to Dragon for me if you see her,' she told him.

'Watch this, Gran,' said Ginny as she stepped out of the doorway, and she threw Egg upwards towards the sky as she had seen racing-pigeon owners do with their birds. But

Egg was no dull grey bird with clumsy clattering wings. Egg was magnificent. Ginny held on tight to the ball of string as Egg soared with slow easy beats of his beautiful wings. The bright sunshine glowed through his wings and lit up his array of colours but it glowed on through the wings so that Ginny could see the shapes of the clouds moving in the sky behind him.

'Isn't he wonderful?' she asked and Gran didn't say anything. She just nodded and waved, her mouth tight closed. Ginny looked back and saw the sunlight glinting on Gran's brooch and on shiny eyes before the door closed.

Chapter Seventeen
EGGSTRAORDINARY

Ginny walked up the road, letting the string unravel in her hands as Egg gained height.

'Don't pull!' she called to him.

He could easily pull the string from her hand if he wanted to. He was big enough and strong enough. He could burn through the string with one hot blast of breath if he wanted to, but he didn't. He rose gently and steadily, circling upwards in the buffeting wind. His scales glinted and sparkled like pale sequins and Ginny watched with a mixture of pride and sadness lumping in her throat.

The only person that they met close up in the short distance between the two homes was the milkman. He took Ginny by surprise because he stopped his milk float outside Gran's house.

'Hello,' he said. 'Your gran asked me to leave milk again today. She said she'd be going home.' And then the milkman noticed Egg. 'What's that, then? A stunt kite?'

Ginny looked up. Egg, bored with waiting while the milkman chatted, was doing loop the loops at the end of his string. She wondered what she could say that would make the milkman lose interest.

'It's a Chinese New Year kite,' she began, but the milkman wasn't listening. He had one hand shading his eyes and his mouth was open in wonder.

'That's extraordinary!' he said. 'I've never seen anything like that – it looks exactly as if it's alive!'

Ginny froze. Had he said *Egg*straordinary? Had he said *Egg*sactly? Did he know?

'Heck,' said the milkman, 'I'd swear that was a real dragon on the end of that string.'

He began to reach for the string as if he were going to pull Egg down out of the sky and Ginny unfroze fast. She pulled the string around so that Egg had the sun directly behind him. The milkman scrunched his eyes up but still had to look away from the dazzling brightness. And at the same moment Ginny kicked at the three empty bottles by Gran's doorstep and sent them noisily rolling towards the road. Rubbing dazzled eyes, the milkman chased after the bottles and Ginny slipped through the side gate to Gran's garden.

The garden was strangely quiet. The hens were cowering in the sooty hen house as if they were afraid of some unseen threat. It made Ginny nervous. They can feel the mother dragon coming, she thought. The air in Gran's garden seemed different from the gusty wind in the street. It was still, still and silent, and the light was different too. She looked up and knew that Egg could feel that something was about to happen. He had stopped his aerobatics and hung in the air above Ginny, slowly beating his wings to keep himself airborne.

'Egg, come here!' She began to pull in the long length of the string. Now that it was about to happen, Ginny was suddenly afraid of the mother dragon in a way that she hadn't been since the fire. She wanted to hide.

As Egg flapped gently down Ginny bundled the string into her pouch pocket and took him into her arms. She looked around the garden, searching for a place where they could hide.

It was too far to go to the house and the climbing trees were still bare of leaves. They would have to hide in the hen house with the hens. There was fresh clean straw inside the hut but the smell of fire was still strong as Ginny opened the door. She hesitated for a moment. It seemed odd to shelter in a place where she had fought a battle so recently, but it didn't feel threatening now. As Egg eagerly watched the sky Ginny knew that he would soon be gone and she would be alone. She quite welcomed the company of the hens.

'Chicken yourself!' she mocked.

Down on her knees in the prickly straw, Ginny undid Egg from the tangle of silk scarves. She put a protective arm around him and wished that she could think of the right things to say to him in their last minutes together. Egg seemed content as he leaned against Ginny and she stroked down his neck

and chest and tried not to think of how much she was going to miss him. The colours of his scales seemed brighter. Even in the dim light coming through the soot-darkened window, they glowed their colours. Ginny picked Egg up and held him gently to her. She had the feeling that if she let go now he would just float up and away.

'You're ready, aren't you,' she whispered and felt tears threatening. Crying would spoil things. She must think about something else.

Ginny looked around her at the blackened hen house. Six pairs of beady yellow eyes watched her as she clung to Egg. She picked up a burnt stick and wrote 'Ginny luvs Egg' on the hen-house wall. But the writing would fade. She wished that she could think of something better, something beautiful to mark her love for the little dragon. She pushed open the door a little way and looked out into the garden, hoping for an idea.

As she looked into the garden, the stick dropped from her hand. 'Egg,' she whispered, 'she's nearly here!'

Chapter Eighteen
THEY BELONG

The garden had changed. The light was different. Over towards Easter Hill the sky was dark and wept heavy rain, but in Gran's garden it was brilliantly, almost glaringly, sunny. Between the two weathers a huge double rainbow arched like a doorway. The wind had gone completely now. Everything was still, still and waiting.

'Listen!' whispered Ginny.

Egg put his head on one side and as he listened he quivered with excitement. A distant beating noise was getting steadily louder. Wings, big wings, thought Ginny. She rested her cheek on the top of Egg's head.

'This is it, Egg.'

They watched through the hen-house doorway as a dark dot in the sky got steadily bigger. Soon Ginny could see the wings flapping on either side of the dot and she began to feel the air buffeted from them as the dragon got nearer. Impatiently she pushed her blown hair away from her eyes, determined not to miss anything. The sound and sight of the large spoked wings flapping startled Ginny with a memory of how Grandad, before he got ill, used to flap his big dark umbrella in the doorway when he came in out of the rain. As the mother dragon flew out of the dull rainy sky and into the bright sunlight of Gran's garden, Ginny could see her properly at last. She was no monster.

'She's beautiful, Egg!' Ginny whispered. 'She's like you!'

The mother dragon was dark bottle green, with scales sparkling purple-blue, grey-green. She was iridescent like a magpie feather, but more so, magically more so. She was big but, like Egg, somehow insubstantial.

'She's lovely,' Ginny whispered to Egg. 'She's got kind eyes like Gran's.'

As she neared the ground the mother dragon stopped beating her wings. She held them steady and the air and noise around Ginny stilled. She glided noiselessly down

onto the grass and lifted up her head. She looked at Ginny standing in the doorway of the hut, and Ginny had the feeling that she could see all her thoughts and secrets with those deep dark eyes. Ginny looked back. But there was something in those eyes that surprised Ginny. The mother dragon was unsure that Ginny would give her baby back, unsure that Egg would even want to go back! Ginny couldn't bear it. She loosened her hold on Egg.

'He'll come!' she called softly to the mother dragon. 'I won't stop him.'

Still the mother dragon didn't move.

'Go on, Egg. It's all right. Go to your mum.'

Egg struggled and Ginny realised that he was still tied to the string. She pulled a piece of the string between her two hands. It cut into her hands but didn't break so she put it between her teeth and bit through it.

Egg scrabbled clumsily through the doorway. He flap-ran straight to the dragon mother who lifted a vast webbed wing to bring him to her.

As they met both dragons sang, Egg his ringing high-up chime and the mother dragon a deeper, more resonant changing chord, but together. Ginny shivered slightly now that the warmth of Egg had gone from her. She nursed the hand cut by the string and watched as the two dragons, big and little, touched noses. Egg's colours glowed brighter than Ginny had ever seen them before. He squeaked one of his high up-and-down questioning squeaks and put his head on one side. The mother dragon sang deep

and steadily like a cathedral organ and smiled down at him. They belonged. Ginny felt left out, but Egg was happy.

When the mother dragon looked towards Ginny again, her eyes seemed to invite Ginny to come closer and be a part of the dragon family for one last time.

'Yes,' said Ginny softly, 'I will.' She walked out of the cold dark hut. The mother dragon lifted her wing again and Ginny stepped under and let its warmth and shelter canopy over her and Egg. Sounds and sights from outside were all muffled and for a few moments it felt as though she and Egg were the only creatures in the world. Egg came up to the height of Ginny's knees now, and she crouched down as he looked up at her with his dark eyes and hummed happiness into her chest. 'Goodbye, Egg,' she said. That was all. And then she let go.

A double chording chime of high and low dragon voices called a message back to her and quite suddenly the safe darkness lifted and a cold wind punched at Ginny as the two dragons lifted up into the sky. Ginny shaded

her eyes to watch as mother and child rose up, circled overhead and saluted her with dipped wings before speeding off fast towards the sun. She watched them get smaller and melt together as the sunlight made her eyes water.

'Come back!' she called, but not loudly.

Ginny rubbed her eyes and looked again, but her eyes filled with tears now and she couldn't see anything moving in the sky except smudged white pigeons flying over the garden. She couldn't hear anything except the hens fussing their way back out into their pen.

As Ginny stood and watched, cloud blotted out the sunlight and it began to rain. Her arms felt strangely empty, but there was something smooth and warm that she unthinkingly turned over and over between her fingers. She folded her fingers around the object. Then, with rain and tears streaming down her face, she ran home. Egg had his mum now and Ginny wanted hers.

Chapter Nineteen
OWEN STEPHEN ABBOT

As Ginny neared home she could see Mum with Gran in the kitchen. She paused for a moment, half-hidden by a tree, and felt the wetness on her face and knew that there were sooty smudges on her jacket. If it had just been Gran in the kitchen then Ginny would have gone to her, but she couldn't go to Mum in this state without all sorts of complicated explanations. She wished that she could.

Ginny crept round to the back door. She dropped her dirty jacket by the washing machine and then went up to her room. She shut the door, shutting out the sound of happy chatter that came from the kitchen. She went to the window and looked out towards Gran's garden and the big sky beyond. It was full of rain clouds now. There was no sun to show which direction the dragons had gone. And no dragons. No Egg.

Ginny clenched her fists tight.

'Ow!' she cried out in surprise and pain as one hand felt a sharp edge inside the fist. She had forgotten that she had something in her hand. Ginny uncurled her fingers and looked down at a slim silky smooth shiny disc that glinted at her. It was a dark bottle-green colour but had dark rainbow colours hidden in the green that came and went as she tilted it to and fro in the light.

Like Gran's mother-of-pearl, only darker, thought Ginny and then she laughed. 'Mother-of-Egg!' It was one of the scales from Egg's mother. Now I have got something to keep for ever, something to

remind me of Egg. She wondered whether this scale was like Egg's and would show its colours more brightly when it was wet. She decided to try it in the bathroom.

As Ginny opened her bedroom door she heard a small noise that wasn't chatter from Gran and Mum. It wasn't even from downstairs, she realised. She stood still to listen and heard again a high-up little voice that sounded something like 'Lair'.

Hardly daring to hope, Ginny stepped into the little bedroom next to hers.

'Oh!' she said in disappointment. The baby's cot was still empty, but 'Lair!' said a little voice by her feet and she looked down to see her little brother, eyes wide open, snugly nestled in a baby car seat on the floor.

'Hello, hedgehog!' Ginny whispered, wanting to keep him to herself. She crouched down beside him and kissed his tickly soft hair. A fat baby fist bumped her nose and she offered a finger. The baby clenched it hard. In her other hand Ginny still had her mother-of-Egg scale. She held it up and tilted it to and fro. The baby's hazy eyes watched

and his legs wiggled happily under their blanket wrapping. 'I'll tell you all about Egg one day,' she told him. 'Perhaps he will come back and you will meet him after all.'

There was the sound of the front door opening and then Dad's voice, 'Who's for fish and chips then? Is our Ginny back yet, or should I put this lot in the oven to keep warm?'

'I noticed her jacket by the back door,' Gran was saying. 'I think that you may well find her if you go upstairs, Maggie. Stephen and I will put things out on the table.'

Then there was the sound of Mum's footsteps running fast up the stairs.

'Ginny?'

Ginny peeped round the door.

'Ginny!' Mum's smile threatened to swallow her ears and she was laughing. 'Well, what do you think?' she asked as she put an arm round Ginny's shoulders and they looked together at the baby.

'Is the baby home for good?' Ginny asked.

'For good and for ever!' said Mum firmly. 'And he's not just "the baby" any more. He is Owen Stephen Abbot. Do you like it?'

'Owen like Grandad,' said Ginny. 'Yes.'

For a little while Ginny and Mum just looked down and smiled, and then Ginny said, 'He looks different. Do you think that's because he's got a name?'

Mum laughed. 'Perhaps that is part of it, but it's his clothes too. He's in coloured clothes now instead of the white hospital T-shirt and blanket.'

Then Mum told Ginny about how she and Dad had walked up Easter Hill and decided that it was time to bring the baby home.

'I cried,' she told Ginny. 'I cried for the first time since Owen was born. I think that the wind and rain blew and washed away something during that walk. That and talking. Anyway, we decided that we wanted our baby home and we wanted to do it straight away. We didn't think to go home first for baby clothes or a car seat, but the nurses lent us this funny egg-shaped seat and Gran had left a bag of baby clothes in case we might need them. My mum has always known me better than I know myself!' Mum laughed.

Ginny had to think for a moment before she realised that Mum was talking about Gran.

'Owen fell asleep in the car on the way home so we left him sleeping in his seat rather than disturb him by putting him in his cot. So, yours was the first face that he saw at home!'

Ginny looked at Owen. He was asleep again, his mouth open and gently snoring.

'Come on,' said Mum. 'Let's eat those fish and chips before he wakes up.'

Chapter Twenty
GREAT TREASURE

That afternoon when Owen was asleep in his cot and Dad was digging the garden, Mum sat down with Ginny.

'Here, have a look at what I've been doing to our patchwork,' she said. She stretched out the bright patchwork of coloured memories and pointed to a new patch. It was the one patch that wasn't colourful.

'Oh,' said Ginny and then 'Oh!' as she recognised the dull whitish material with a bit of black writing on one corner. 'The hospital T-shirt! A patch for Owen! Oh good!'

'It's a bit dull,' said Mum. 'But it's still special.' She smiled. 'The nurse let me take it.' And then the smile went and Mum looked intently at Ginny. 'Sometimes it's the dull things, the ordinary things that are most important in life, Gin. That patch will always be very special to me.'

'And me,' said Ginny and she looked at Mum's serious face. 'Mum, can I tell you something?' she asked. Was it a good idea to tell? She did want Mum to know.

Mum nodded and so Ginny told her all about Egg. By the end of the telling Ginny had tears running down her face and Mum's arms hugged around her. 'Egg sounds very special,' she said. 'I'm glad that he was here for you when I wasn't. It was a strange time for me too, Gin. When Owen was born handicapped I didn't know what to think or do. I just wanted to huddle into a safe shell away from everything. And now, well, I suppose I've hatched out into a world that is different from the one I was used to but still one that I can be happy in. Very happy.' She gave Ginny a tight squeeze. 'Can you understand any of that?' Ginny nodded. 'Good,' said Mum, sitting up properly and reaching for the sewing box. 'Then let's finish off this patchwork and turn it into a quilt to keep our little Owen warm and snug.'

'OK,' said Ginny. 'You know, Egg was

bright colours like the quilt when he was happy.'

Mum raised her eyebrows. 'He must have been very beautiful. Could you draw Egg for me?'

So Ginny got out pens and paper and drew a little dragon with a green snub nose and multi-coloured scales running from its head, down its back and along its tail. She drew wonderful webbed wings and a soft green underbelly. Then she drew two deep dark eyes that seemed to look right through her. She showed the picture to Mum.

'Do you know,' said Mum, 'he reminds me

of something,' and she ran a finger down the little picture dragon's back. 'He's almost familiar. I wonder where I could have seen him before?' Mum shook her head and went back to threading her needle. 'Perhaps it'll come back to me,' she said.

'I hope that he comes back to me,' said Ginny.

When Owen woke up, Mum lifted him gently out of his cot. 'Hello, my treasure,' she said.

Treasure, thought Ginny, 'great treasure'. Dragons guard great treasure.

Gran saw Ginny frowning. 'You're looking broody again, Gin! What is it this time?'

Ginny just shook her head slightly and smiled.

'Well,' said Gran looking at them all. 'It seems that everyone is back where they should be except me. I think it's time I got back home to my silly hens.'

'But will you help us do "Bottoms" first?' asked Ginny. 'We need you to hold Owen.'

Dad laughed. 'You don't really want to do

that old thing, do you, Gin?'

But Mum replied for her. 'Yes,' she said firmly, 'we do.' She handed Owen to Gran and they did it.

'Daddy "A" bot, Mummy "B" bot,
Ginny "C" bot and Owen "D" bot,'
Mum sang, 'We've got one *more*,
so now we're *four* bottoms',

and Gran twiddled baby Owen round to bump his tiny nappied bottom and be hugged into the family circle. Ginny hugged Mum, Dad and Owen hard and closed her eyes for a moment. And Egg is 'E' bot, she thought. I mustn't ever forget him.